P9-DEB-248

For Niki, with love

ABOUT THE STORY

This is a traditional Irish folktale, International Tale Type 510, Type 403 appendage, Aarne Thompson.
It is reproduced in <u>Myths and Folk Tales of Ireland</u> by Jeremiah Curtin (Dover Publications, 1975)
and <u>The Penguin Book of Irish Folktales</u>, ed. Henry Glassie (Penguin, 1993)

Copyright © 2000 by Jude Daly
By arrangement with The Inkman, Cape Town, South Africa
Hand-lettering by Andrew van der Merwe
First published in Great Britain by Frances Lincoln Limited, 2000
Printed in China
First American edition, 2000
Sunburst edition, 2005
1 3 5 7 9 10 8 6 4 2

www.fsgkidsbooks.com

Library of Congress Cataloging-in-Publication Data
Daly, Jude.
    Fair, Brown & Trembling : an Irish Cinderella story / Jude Daly.
        p. cm.
    Summary: This version of the Cinderella story, in which a young girl overcomes the wickedness of her older sisters to become
the bride of a prince, is based on an Irish folktale.
    ISBN-13: 978-0-374-42257-8 (pbk.)
    ISBN-10: 0-374-42257-5 (pbk.)
    [1. Fairy Tales.   2. Folklore—Ireland.]   I. Cinderella. English.   II. Title.   III. Title: Fair, Brown and Trembling.

PZ8.D16Fai   2000
398.2'09417'02
[E]—dc21
                                                                                                      99-34315

FAIR, BROWN & TREMBLING

An Irish Cinderella Story

jude daly

A Sunburst Book

Farrar, Straus and Giroux

Once upon a time, high among the green hills of Erin, there stood a castle. In it lived a widower and his three daughters: Fair, Brown, and Trembling.

Fair and Brown always wore new dresses to church on Sundays. Trembling stayed at home. "You must do the cooking," said her sisters. But the real reason they would not let her out of the house was because Trembling was very beautiful, and they were terrified she would marry before they did.

One Sunday morning, when Fair and Brown had gone to church, the old henwife came into the kitchen. "It's at church you ought to be, young woman!" she said.

"How can I?" said Trembling. "I have only these old clothes. And what if my sisters were to see me there? They'd never let me out again!"

"Well," said the henwife, "you've always been kind to me, so now I'll give you a dress finer than they have ever seen. What will you have?"

Trembling thought this was a splendid game. "Oh," she said, "a dress as white as snow—and green shoes for my feet." The henwife clipped a piece from Trembling's old dress. Then, putting on her cloak of darkness, she muttered some strange words . . .

. . . and, the next moment, she was holding out a lily-white gown and the prettiest pair of shamrock-green shoes you ever did see!

Trembling couldn't believe her eyes. She laughed with delight. Then she dressed herself in her beautiful new clothes.

When she was ready, the henwife led her outside, where a milk-white mare stood saddled and waiting.

"A word of warning," said the old woman. "Do not go inside the church door.
And the moment the service finishes, ride home as fast as the mare will carry you!"
Trembling thanked her. Then she climbed on the mare's back and rode off.

In church that morning, everyone kept turning around to stare at the beautiful young woman standing in the doorway.

As soon as the Mass ended, Trembling hurried away. Some of the young men tried to overtake her as she rode off, but in vain. Trembling outstripped the wind as she galloped home on her milk-white mare.

The henwife had dinner all ready, and by the time her sisters came home,
Trembling was back in her old clothes.

"Have you any news?" asked the henwife.

"Indeed," they replied. "We saw such a fascinating woman at the church door!
All the men—from the king down to the poorest beggar—wanted to meet her.
Her dress was unlike any we have ever seen."

Fair and Brown were impatient to find a dress just the same—but such fine cloth was nowhere to be found in the land of Erin.

The next Sunday, when Fair and Brown had gone to church, the henwife came
in and asked, "Will you go to church today?"

"I would," replied Trembling, "if only I could."

"What will you wear?" said the henwife.

"Oh, the finest black satin," answered Trembling, "with scarlet shoes."

"And what color shall the mare be?" asked the henwife.

"So black and glossy that I can see myself in her coat," said Trembling.

Once more, the henwife put on her cloak of darkness . . . and, the next moment,
she held out a rippling black gown and red shoes to Trembling.

In church, everyone was curious to know who the woman in black at the church door could be. But just as before, Trembling slipped away at the end and was home before any man could stop her. The henwife had dinner ready, and Trembling was back in her old clothes when her sisters got home.

"What news today?" asked the henwife.

"We saw the strange woman again," they said, "and none of the men noticed our dresses—they were all too busy gazing at her!"

Fair and Brown hunted high and low for a black dress just the same—but such finery was not to be found the length and breadth of Erin.

When the third Sunday came, Trembling asked the henwife for a dress with a snow-white bodice and rose-red skirt, and a cape of mossy green. She wore a hat trimmed with red, white, and green plumes, and on her feet were little blue slippers.

That morning, she rode a white mare decorated with blue and gold diamonds.

By now, news of the mysterious young woman had spread far and wide. Princes from north, south, east, and west crowded into the church, each hoping for her hand in marriage.

The Mass ended, and Trembling was already up on her mare, ready to race away ahead of the wind. But the Prince of Emania, who had stayed outside the church during the service, reached out as she passed by and pulled off her slipper.

Trembling rode home faster than ever. When her sisters came home, she was back in her old clothes, hard at work.

"And what news today?" asked the henwife.

"Today," said the sisters, "the strange woman came to the church again. Her dress was even more splendid than before—and such colors! She is the most beautiful woman ever seen in Erin."

The Prince of Emania made an announcement. He proclaimed that he
would marry the lady whose foot fitted the slipper, whoever she might be.
But all the other princes wanted to marry the mysterious woman, too.
"Let us fight for her," they said.
"Very well," replied the Prince of Emania. "But first we must find her."

They traveled all over the land, searching. Many hopeful ladies tried on the little blue slipper. Yet, though it was neither too large nor too small, somehow it never quite fit. One woman even cut a bit off her big toe—but it was no use!

When Fair and Brown heard about the princes' search, they spoke of nothing else. And when Trembling said, "Maybe it's my foot that the slipper will fit," they jeered, "How stupid you are!" Still, when they heard that the princes were coming to their house, they locked Trembling in a cupboard.

The Prince of Emania with his companions came and offered the slipper to each sister in turn. They tried and tried, but it would not fit.

"Are there any other young women in the house?" asked the prince.

"There is one," cried a faint voice from the cupboard.

"Oh, her," said the sisters. "We just keep her to clean up the ashes."

But the princes refused to leave until Trembling had tried on the slipper.

So, unwillingly, the two sisters let Trembling out.

She took the little blue shoe and slipped it on her foot. It fit perfectly!

The Prince of Emania gazed at Trembling, and said, "Yes, it was you I saw outside the church," and everyone agreed that she was the mysterious woman.

"But now we must fight for her," said the other princes.

They went outside. A prince from Lochlin stepped forward, and the struggle began—and what a terrible struggle it was! They fought for nine hours, before the prince from Lochlin gave up his claim and left the field.

Next day, a Spanish prince fought for six hours before yielding his claim.

On the third day, a Zulu prince fought for six hours, then retired, defeated.

But on the fourth day no more princes came forward, and it was decided that Trembling should become the Prince of Emania's bride.

So the Prince and Trembling were married.

In time they had fourteen children, and they lived ever after in great happiness.

As for Fair and Brown . . .

. . . they were put out to sea in a barrel with provisions for seven years—
and were never seen again!